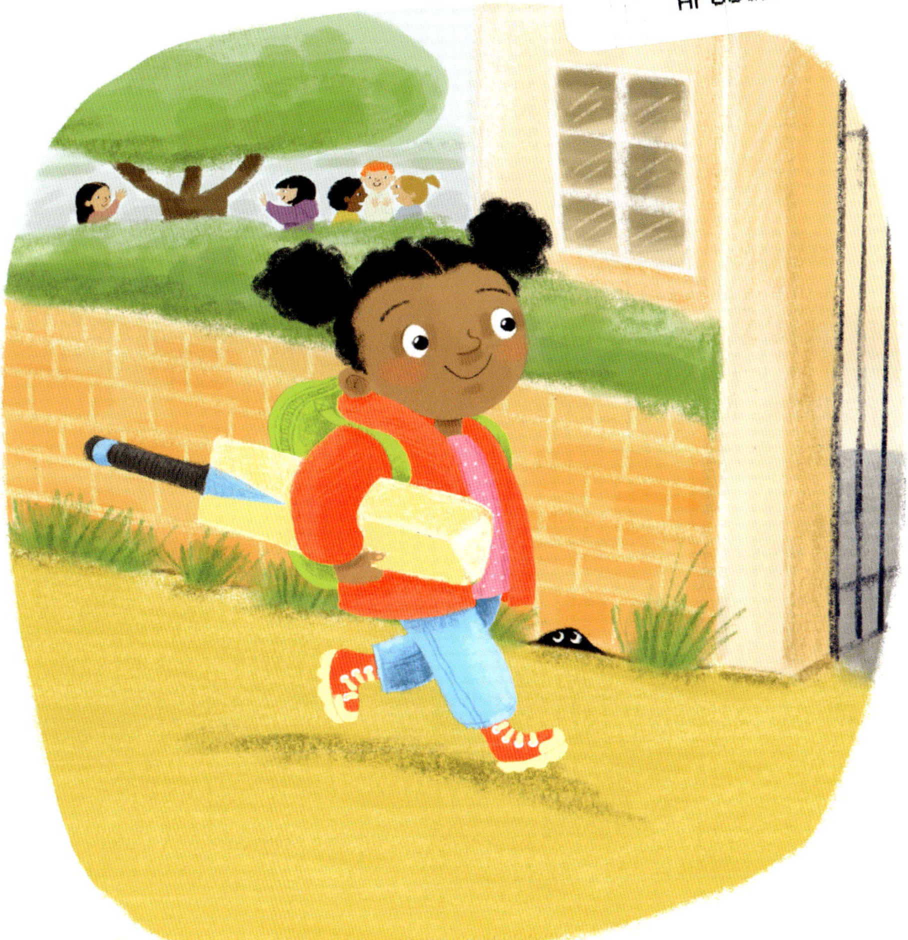

Beth has a bat...

a cricket bat!

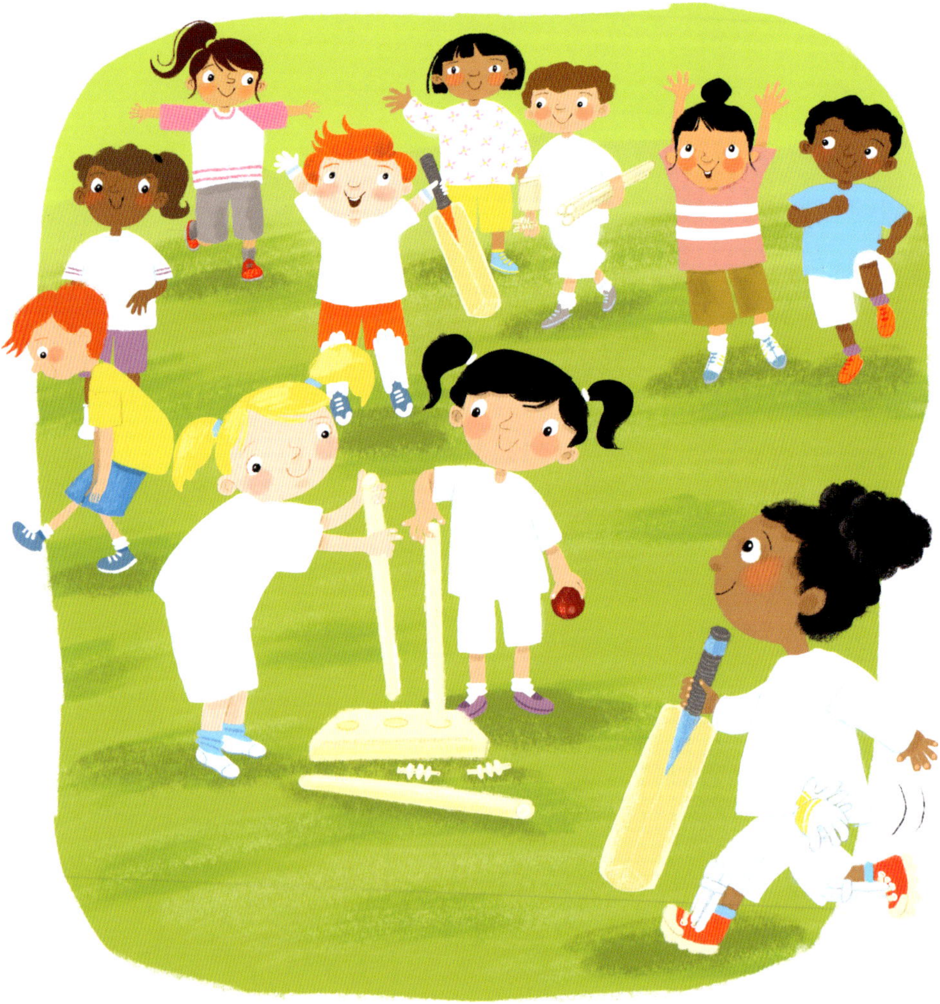

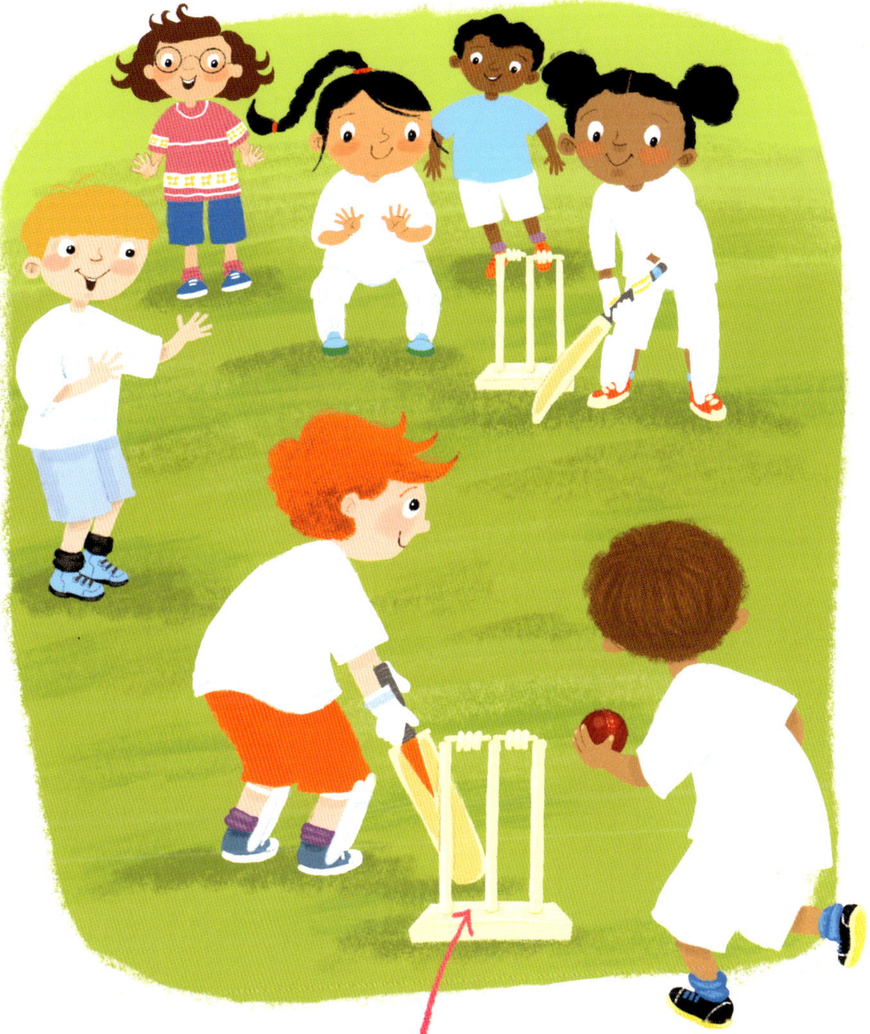

the wicket

Whack!

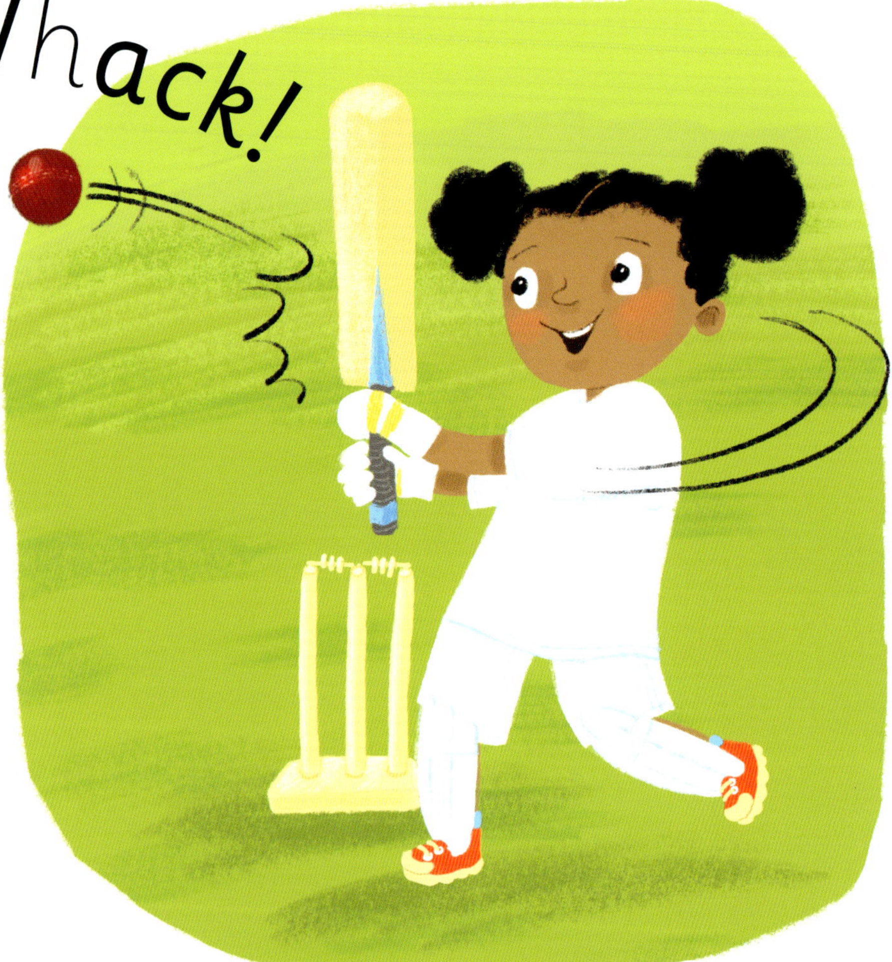

Beth runs.

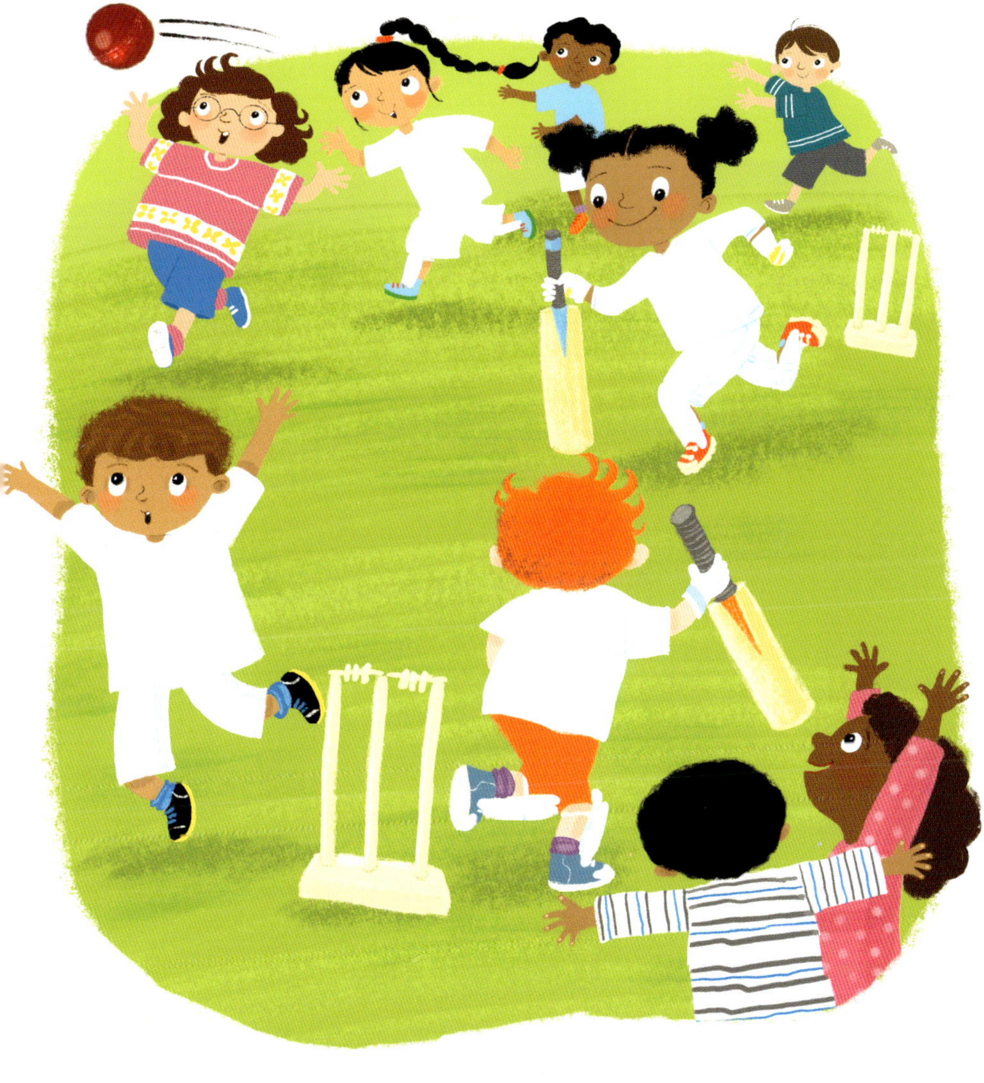

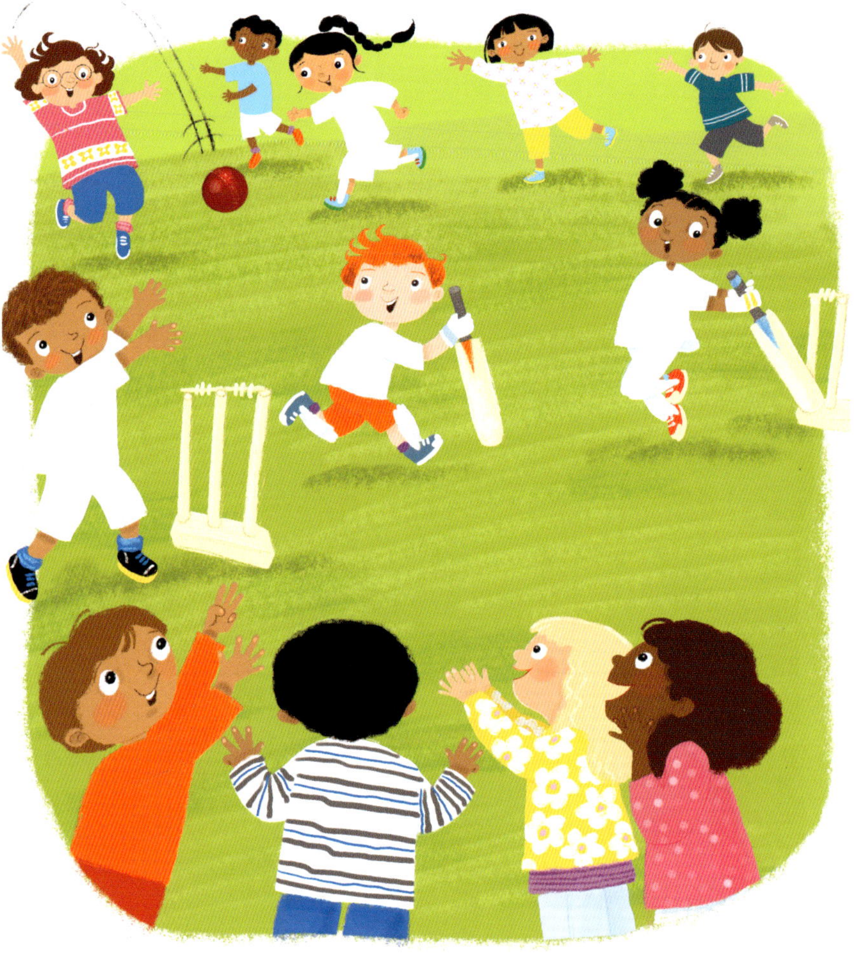

Three runs!

"Stop!" shouts Ben.

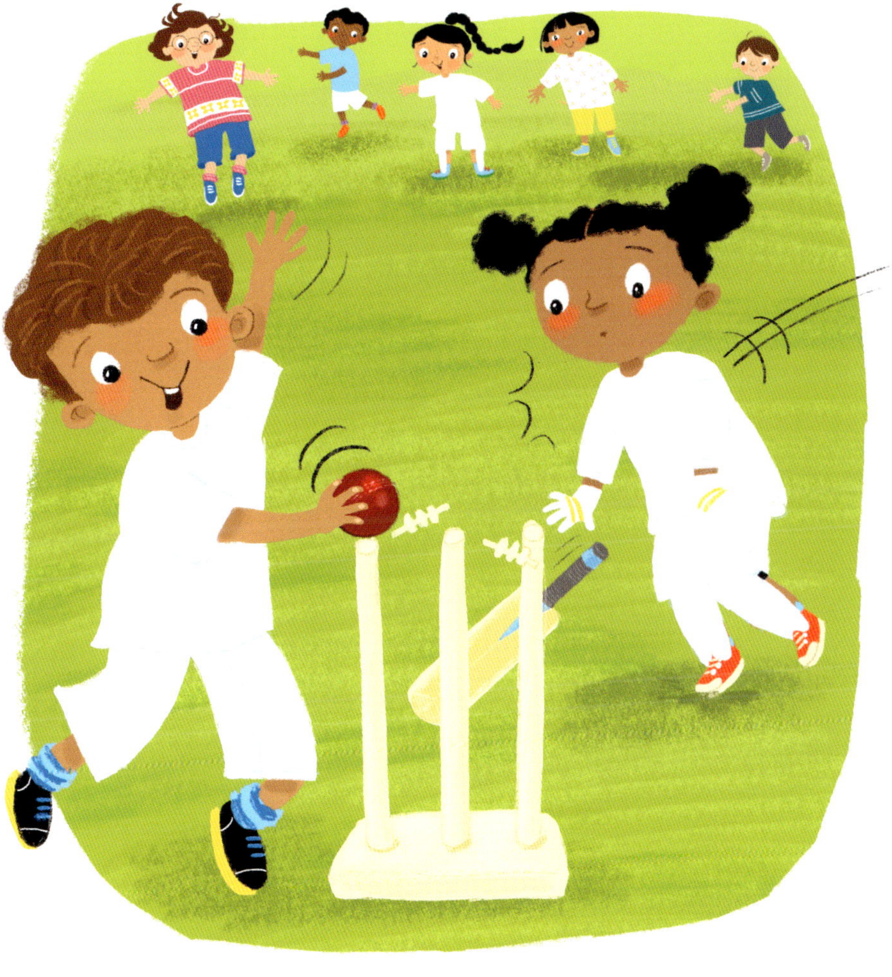

Beth is out.

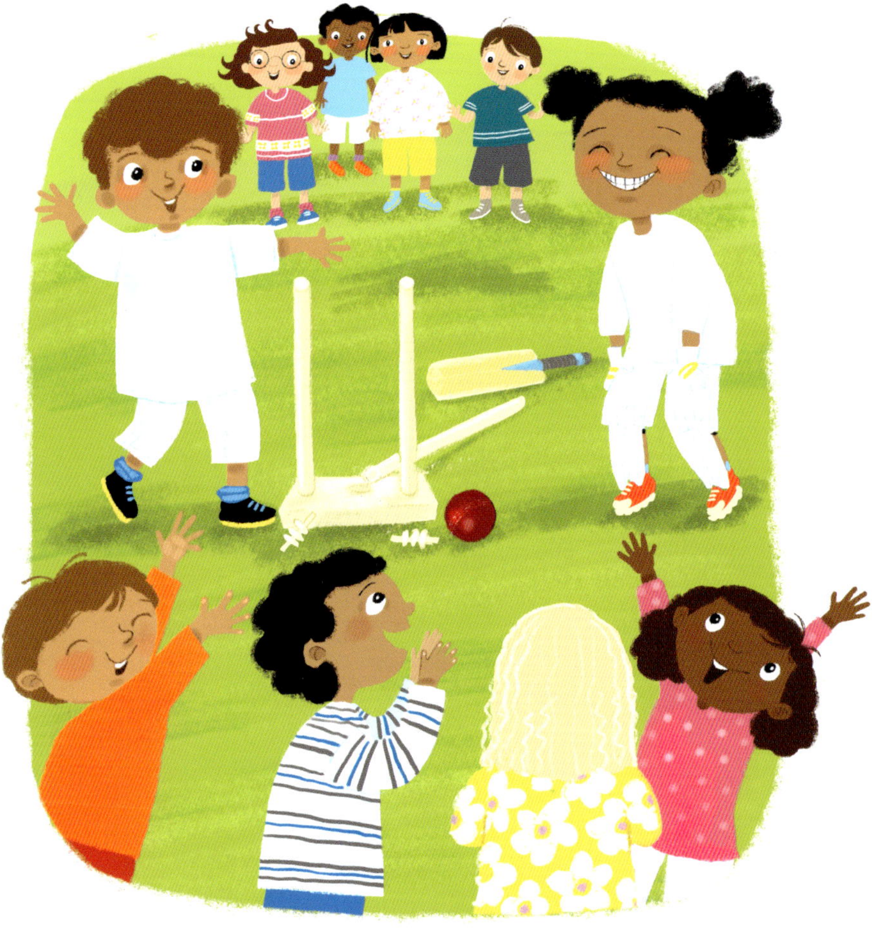

She grins.